The
Ice Castle

For the best bestie
and mountaineer,
Sandeep
—G. S.

DaiSY DReAMER

THe Ice Castle

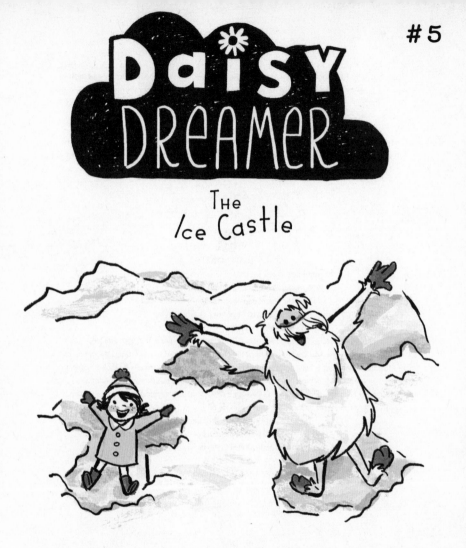

By Holly Anna • Illustrated by Genevieve Santos

LITTLE SIMON

New York London Toronto Sydney New Delhi

LITTLE SIMON

An imprint of Simon & Schuster Children's Publishing Division

1230 Avenue of the Americas, New York, New York 10020

First Little Simon paperback edition November 2017

Copyright © 2017 by Simon & Schuster, Inc.

Also available in a Little Simon hardcover edition.

All rights reserved, including the right of reproduction in whole or in part in any form.

LITTLE SIMON is a registered trademark of Simon & Schuster, Inc., and associated colophon is a trademark of Simon & Schuster, Inc. For information about special discounts for bulk purchases, please contact Simon & Schuster Special Sales at 1-866-506-1949 or business@simonandschuster.com. The Simon & Schuster Speakers Bureau can bring authors to your live event. For more information or to book an event contact the Simon & Schuster Speakers Bureau at 1-866-248-3049 or visit our website at www.simonspeakers.com.

Designed by Laura Roode

Manufactured in the United States of America 1017 MTN

2 4 6 8 10 9 7 5 3 1

This book has been cataloged with the Library of Congress.

ISBN 978-1-4814-9893-7 (hc)

ISBN 978-1-4814-9892-0 (pbk)

ISBN 978-1-4814-9894-4 (eBook)

CONTENTS

☆ CHAPTER ONE ☆

Happy Snow Day!

WHOOSH!

A gust of wind whips the covers off my warm, snuggly bed. Does the wind want to play hide-and-seek? I feel around for sheets and blankets. I am like a grumpy caterpillar that wants to stay inside her cocoon. I tug the covers over my head.

SWOOSH!

The wind steals them again!

"BAAAAH!" I cry as I jerk the covers back over me. Sir Pounce attacks the ripples in my blanket. "STOP!" Then I scrunch up in a ball to keep warm. It's freezing in here. And, wait, *why* is there *wind* in my *bedroom*?

I peek out from under my covers and do a double blink. *Am I dreaming?* I wonder. Or maybe my eyeballs are playing tricks on me! Because . . .

It's *snowing!*

In. My. Room.

And there is an *igloo!*

On. My. Floor.

And someone is crawling out of the igloo's tunnel right now, and I know just who it is! Posey! My imaginary friend!

"HAPPY SNOW DAY!" he shouts, a proud smile on his face. I rub my eyes and smile back at him. Only Posey could make it snow in my room. Then my imaginary friend hops to the window.

"It's snowing outside, too!" he exclaims.

I want to look out and see the snow, but I'm tangled in my covers. I roll right off my bed and onto the floor. *Oof!*

I jump to my feet and brush the snow off my pajamas. *Brrr!* Then I take two large leaps to the window. *Yeow!* My feet are like ice cubes! But I look outside anyway. The snow has frosted the lawn, the fence, the bird feeder, and all the limbs on the trees.

"It's our first snow day together!" I say, dancing from one foot to the other to avoid the cold.

Posey has already started to roll a ball for a snowman right on my bedroom floor! I want to help him, but my feet are frozen, and—oh no!—I hear footsteps on the stairs.

I tap Posey's shoulder like a woodpecker.

"Posey! My mom is coming!" I warn him. "Make it stop snowing in here! Get rid of that igloo! *HURRY!* Or I'll be sent to the North Pole for real!"

☆ ✩ CʜᴀᴘᴛᴇR Two ☆

Zoom! Zoom! Zoom!

"What's the big deal?" Posey asks as he stands in the middle of the snow—*in my room*—doing absolutely *nothing*. "Doesn't your mom like snow days?"

I lock my door to buy time.

"Of course she likes them!" I explain. "But not *inside the house*! It doesn't snow *inside* in the real world. Only *outside*!"

Posey runs to my desk and pulls out a pad of paper. He draws a picture of the sun—like that's going to help! Then he floats up and grabs hold of my ceiling fan with one hand. "Turn it on and let the sun shine!" he calls.

I flip the switch, and *ZOOMIE! ZOOM! ZOOOOOOM!*

Rays of light burst from Posey's drawing as he spins in circles. His sun is melting the snow!

HURRY! HURRY! I think, trying to make the snow melt faster. Because now my mom is *knocking on my door!*

"Just a sec!" I call. I wait for the sun to melt everything—the snow, the igloo, and every last drop of leftover water. Then Posey plops to the floor and dives right under my bed. I unlock the door like nothing's going on. Mom pokes her head in.

"Whew!" she exclaims, fanning her face. "It feels like an oven in here! I'd better turn down the heat!"

The piece of paper with Posey's sun floats gently down behind her. She doesn't notice.

"Good news," Mom says as she continues. "School has been called off. It's a *snow* day!"

I'm still freaked out about what just went on in my room, so I act surprised. "Snow?" I say. "What snow?"

Mom laughs. "Silly sleepyhead!" she says. "Just look outside! It's been snowing all night. We *both* have the day off!"

I pump my fists. "That's spectacular news!" I say.

Mom picks up Posey's sun picture

on her way to the door. "If you clean up your room, we can play in the snow," she says. "How does that sound?"

That sounds very *cool* to me.

CHA-BANG-A!

Posey scrambles out from under my bed. "Great snowflakes, that was *close*!"

I untangle the blankets to make my bed. "Too close," I say.

Posey looks out the window. "Look, it's snowing even harder now!" he says, changing the subject. "I doubt you'll be able to go out and play anytime soon. Unless . . ."

I pull up my bedspread. "Unless what?" I ask curiously.

"Unless you want to see what a snow day is like in the World of Make-Believe?"

I plump my pillows. "Of course I want to see what it's like!" *Obviously.*

Posey spins in a circle. "Well, what are we waiting for?" he says. "Let's *go!*"

I quickly change into warm clothes. Posey grabs my erasable marker from off my desk. This time he draws a door on my *floor*. *Seriously?* He pulls on the handle. The door doesn't open. Then we both tug on it. It still won't budge.

"The door must be frozen shut!" Posey exclaims. "Let's stomp on it!"

Posey jumps on it first. It doesn't budge.

Then we both jump on the door at the same time.

CHA-BANG-A! The door swings open like a trap, and we fall right through. My pigtails stick straight up as we rocket down through the sky.

"Aim for a bed!" Posey shouts.

The wind whistles in my ears.

"A bed?"

Far below I can see all kinds of beds on the ground: a sleigh bed, a canopy bed, a four-poster bed, a pirate ship bed. . . . Then I spy a bed with pink daisies on it.

Chilly snow cones! I'm coming in *fast*. I waggle my legs and flap my arms to help steer my body. Then I squeeze my eyes shut just before landing.

CHAPTER FOUR

Bed-Sledding

FLUMP!

I crash into deep fluff. The bedding is so soft and plush, it doesn't even kinda-sorta hurt. *Ahhhhh,* I could lie here all day. But then I realize I'm moving and swirling.

"WHOA!" I shout as I spin down a ginormous hill.

I hold on to the sides of the bed

for dear life. Then a bright purple bird flies alongside me.

"I've never seen bed-sledding like *that* before!" says the bird.

The bedcovers are flapping like crazy.

"Is that what this is called?" I shout to the bird. "Bed-sledding?"

The bird flaps closer and answers me. "That's right! Hold the covers and steer. It's like riding a bike!"

Riding a bike? This is nothing like riding a bike! I think.

"What do you know about riding a bike, Mr. Bird?" I ask.

"NOTHING!" he tweets as he zooms off. "I'm a bird! Birds don't ride bikes!"

Well, that is no help! I guess I'll just have to figure this out myself.

I roll over and sit up in the bed-sled. Then I grab the corners of the quilt like handles and steady myself. The bed-sled seems to respond. I pull tighter and stop spinning. It's better, except there's a hill in front of me that looks like a giant ski jump.

Uh-oh!

I sail high over the jump. And then my giant bed-sled starts to *fly*! *"WOOOOO-HOOOOO!"*

I'm soaring over the WOM! The sun sparkles on the snow beneath me. Wow, this must be what it's like to be inside a diamond ring.

My pillows and blankets poof up as I drift back to the ground. As I glide down another hill, Posey pulls up beside me. His bed-sled looks like a sports car.

He pumps his eyebrows at me. "Looks like you picked a real *winter* of a bed-sled!"

"Don't you mean a real *winner*?" I ask. "That's how you're supposed to say it." *Obviously.*

Posey shakes his head firmly. "When you pick a good bed-sled, we call it a real *winter*," he explains.

"That's because *winter* is the best time to bed-sled."

We launch off of another hilltop, and I can see some of the places I've visited before, like Moonstur Hollow and the Golly Ghost town.

I'm so busy looking around that I don't watch where I'm going. My bed-sled slows to a stop and I teeter on the edge of a cliff.

"Wait! Daisy, don't go down that way!" Posey calls after me. "That will lead you to the Ice Castle!" His voice trails off as he bed-sleds into the distance. I'm all alone.

The snow crunches beneath me. I jump to the back of the bed-sled to keep myself from tipping over. But it's no use. The snow gives way, and my bed-sled takes off. I'm heading into a bobsled chute! I slide down icy curves

and snuggle up for a
wild ride.

SHOOOOOOOOSH! SHOOOOOOOSH!
SHOOOOOOOSH!

Finally I slow down and come to a stop. My pigtails have come undone, and my hair covers my face. *Patooie!* I blow it out of my face, and now I can see again. And oh, what a sight!

I'm sitting right in front of a real
live frozen-to-goodness Ice Castle.

CHAPTER FIVE

Snow-nimals

"Wooooow!" I exclaim as I jump off my bed-sled. "A castle made completely of ice!" It has crystal ice towers, ice-brick walls, and an ice drawbridge. It is magical.

Suddenly the snow around me starts to move. *That's weird.* The white ground wiggles and rolls into snow-balls. Then they each roll toward me.

They look like fluffy white bowling balls. I back away a little, and when I do, the snowballs begin to pop.

POP! POOF! POP! POOF!

Each snowball turns into a tiny snow animal! A snow bunny! A snow polar bear! A snow fox! A snow raccoon! And what else can I say? "Hello! You are *So. Mega. Cute!*"

"*Shhhhhhh!*" they say.

Hmm, that's rude. I have no idea why these snow creatures are shushing me! I can't *stand* being shushed.

"You must be quiet!" whispers the polar bear.

I frown because now I'm a little annoyed. "Why? And who are you?"

The snow penguin shuffles closer. "We're Snow-nimals," he says in a soft voice. "Our job is to make sure the only sound near the Ice Castle is the sound of falling snow."

That makes me wonder, *What does falling snow sound like?* So I stand really still and listen. And guess what? Falling snow has no sound at all! It's like having on earmuffs.

"It is a beautiful, deep quiet," I whisper.

The Snow-nimals all nod at the same time, and they look like snowy bobbleheads. I try not to giggle, but a little snort slips out. *"Honka!"*

The Snow-nimals shush me again. *Obviously.*

"Does anyone live in there?" I ask.

But before I get an answer, Posey slides beside me.

"Um, you were supposed to stay away from the Ice Castle!" he whispers loudly.

I point to my bed-sled. "Tell that to this thing," I say. It is definitely the bed-sled's fault, and it's also a little Posey's fault for not giving me a bed-sledding lesson. "And why didn't you warn me?"

"Everyone knows about the Ice Castle," says Posey.

"Not me!" I say a little too loud. The Snow-nimals all flinch.

"Oh, never mind," Posey whispers. "Let's just move a safe distance away." He points to a field.

We leave our bed-sleds behind by the castle and head for the clear, white meadow.

The Snow-nimals pop back into balls and roll beside us.

Posey gives me a sly smile on the way. "Do you know how to make a snow-berang?"

"A what?" I ask as we trudge along.

"You'll see," Posey whispers.

Then I look back over my shoulder. *What I really want to see is the inside of that Ice Castle,* I think.

☆ Chapter Six ☆

Snow-berang Fight!

Posey and I start a surprise race to the meadow. We playfully nudge each other the rest of the way.

Then *WHOMP!* Posey pushes me off balance, and I splat face-first in the snow. It's like landing in soft powdered sugar that's really, really cold!

"I never knew you liked snow so much!" he teases.

I dust myself off and make a face at him. I quickly make a snowball and chuck it at Posey. It explodes softly against his back. That makes me feel somewhat better.

"So what's a snow-berang, any-how?" I ask again.

Posey scoops a clump of snow and sculpts it into a stretched out V—just like a boomerang. He holds it out in front of me.

"*This* is a snow-berang," he says.

Then Posey holds it by one end and throws it into the air. *Zing!* The snow-berang twirls away from us. Then—*zap!*—it comes right back to him.

"Boomer-awesome! My turn! My turn!" I cheer.

Posey hands me the snow-berang. Now, throwing a boomerang is hard. But throwing a snow-berang is harder, apparently. As soon as I fling it into the air, it crumbles apart. I have to try again and again until I finally get a snow-berang to come back to me.

"Now that you've got the hang of it, let's have a snow-berang fight!" Posey says.

We divide into two teams. Posey is a captain of one team, and I am the captain of the other. The Snownimals are super excited to play too! They are great at making a stockpile of snow-berangs. And they can make them fast!

"Ready? Set! GO!" Posey yells.

Snow-berangs fly through the air. Every time someone gets hit, they have to go out. It's just like a snow-ball fight in the Real World, except the snow-berangs can go in two directions!

I dive behind a mound of snow and poke my head out when I'm ready to throw.

ZING! SPLAT! POOF!
ZING! SPLAT! POOF!

Soon everyone is out except Posey and me. We are both hiding.

"No fair!" the Snow-nimals cry. "You can't hide!"

They're right. So Posey and I jump out of our safe spots and hurl our snow-berangs. I duck Posey's throw and stay down because I know that thing is coming back the other way. My throw goes farther than I meant. Posey floats in the air and laughs. "Looks like you missed, Daisy!"

Another second goes by, then . . . *SMACK! My snow-berang hits Posey right in the back of the head!*

"WRONG AGAIN! I WIN!" I yell at the top of my lungs, and my voice echoes all over.

The Snow-nimals turn back into snowballs and roll away. Posey covers his ears. *Oopsy-daisy!* I didn't mean to be so loud.

I'm about to say I'm sorry when— *KABOOM!*—we hear something much, much, much louder than little old me.

"What was that?" I whisper.

Posey shakes his head and looks in the direction of the Ice Castle. "I think you brought down the drawbridge."

☆ CHAPTER SEVEN ☆

The Ice Castle

"I couldn't possibly make enough noise to open an ice drawbridge!" I say. "Could I?"

Posey's eyes grow very large. He doesn't agree. *Obviously.*

I fold my arms. "Oh, come on," I say. "Who lives in there, anyway?"

A Snow-nimal owl pops out of his snowball.

"Who, who, who indeed?" says the owl. "We have no idea. The Ice Castle was built by a king and queen long ago, but it was too cold for them, so they moved. Then we began to hear creepy sounds coming from inside. That castle is who, who, who, *haunted*."

I frown. "Doesn't everybody know there are no such things as *ghosts*?" I say firmly.

"Except for the Golly Ghosts," Posey reminds me.

"Oh yeah. Maybe there *is* a ghost in there," I say.

The owl flutters its wispy white wings. "The castle moans and wails," the owl says, "and nobody ever goes in or comes out."

"That does sounds pretty ghostly." I punch my fist against the palm of my other hand. "Well, I'm going in! Who's coming with me?"

Then I make fresh tracks toward the palace. Posey groans, but I can hear him follow me. He knows I won't take no for an answer. *Clomp! Clomp! Clomp!* I march across the drawbridge and into the great hall.

Oh. My. Snowflakes.

"Posey, look! *Everything* is made of ice!"

A giant staircase rose up to a glittery platform with two ice thrones. Those must be where the king and queen used to sit. There are also pillars carved to look like trees, and there are ice sculptures of woodland creatures

everywhere. Even the furniture is made of ice—sofas, tables, chairs, and a grand piano!

The Snow-nimals peek from the doorway. I wave them over, and they carefully come inside. Posey is not so careful. He runs up the staircase and slides down the banister.

"HELLO-O-O-O?" I shout into the big space. "Is anybody home?" I peer down a long ice hallway. *Oh, if only*

I had skates, I think. Then I'd skate all the way to that door at the end! I take two big steps and slide. Posey slides beside me.

"I think this hallway leads to the tower," he says.

I take two more steps and slide.

"I do love towers!" I say. "I wonder if it has a giant spiral ice staircase." Then I slide right up to the door.

"Hold on, Daisy. What if something *awful* is behind that door?" he asks. "What if this castle really *is* haunted?"

I listen with my ear against the cold door. "Well, I don't hear a thing!" I whisper. Then I turn the knob, open the door, and . . .

SSHHHHWOOOOOSHHH!

A blast of icy wind blows us right off our feet, and we slip-slide on our bottoms down the hall, out the door, and across the drawbridge. The Snow-nimals turn back into snowballs and scatter.

"What was THAT?!" I cry, jumping
to my feet. "Did you see anything?"

Posey scrambles closer to me and
points.

I turn to see where he's pointing
and—*hold on to your snow boots!*—
something is standing in the castle's
doorway. And it's not a ghost. It's *so*
not a ghost.

☆ Chapter Eight ☆

Naklin

And it's *huge*. And it's *furry*. And oh my gosh . . . *It's waving at us! It's a real live abominable snowman!* And it is the cutest, fluffiest thing I've ever seen!

Posey clings to me like a koala bear.

We're gonna be friends with this guy! I think as I walk toward the Ice Castle *wearing* Posey.

The abominable snowman welcomes us in with a nod. He's so big that he accidentally bumps into a bookcase and ice books tumble to the floor. He lets out a deep laugh and picks them up.

"I'm Daisy!" I say, introducing myself and pretending not to notice his clumsiness. "And this is Posey."

"HELLO, DAISY!" he booms in a voice as big as his body. "HELLO, AND-THIS-IS-POSEY," he says, like Posey's name is a whole entire sentence. "MY NAME IS NAKLIN," he goes on. "I'M A YETI."

"Wow, I thought yetis lived in caves!" I blurt out, and I hope this doesn't sound rude.

He laughs, and the ice chandeliers above us jingle. "MOST YETIS DO," he says.

Posey lets go of me and slides to the floor. "Could you speak a little quieter?" he asks. "We wouldn't want to shatter the Ice Castle."

"Sorry," Naklin says in a smaller voice. "It's been a long time since I've spoken to anyone with such little ears."

"Why were you in the tower?" I ask.

Naklin sighs long and low. I can tell this yeti has a story, so Posey and I plop onto an ice sofa to listen.

"I moved in after the king and queen left," he explains. "It was so beautiful and cold—I loved it so much!

Then one day I climbed the tower to see a snow-bow."

Posey pokes me in the side. "A snow-bow is a rainbow made of snow," he whispers in my ear. And of course now I want to see one.

"When I came back down, the door had blown shut," Naklin goes on. "I've been trapped there ever since." He shakes his head at the thought of it.

I pat Naklin's furry arm. "Oh no. How long were you stuck?"

He slumps forward. "Five years," he says sadly. "I was so lonely, even though yetis like to be alone."

"Why didn't you call for help?" Posey asks.

"I did!" says Naklin. "Yetis sing for help like this." Then he lets out a mournful cry that echoes through the snow.

I grab Posey's arm. "That's the creepy sound the Snow-nimals must have been hearing! The castle was never haunted! Naklin was singing!"

Naklin looks down at his ginormous feet. "Oh yes, yetis are not very good at singing," he says.

Posey and I laugh.

But there's still one thing I don't understand.

"The tower door wasn't locked," I say. "Why didn't you just open the door and walk out?"

"Open the door?" he repeats.

"Yes!" I say. *Obviously.* But then I think that maybe a door isn't so obvious to a yeti. Most caves don't have doors, let alone doorknobs. "Hold on," I say. And then I slide to the closest door and show Naklin how it works.

"THIS MEANS I COULD HAVE GOTTEN OUT THE WHOLE TIME?" Naklin realizes loudly. He bangs his forehead with his paw.

"Well, now you know!" I say, not wanting him to feel like a total silly-head. Then I have an idea. "Want to come play in the snow with us?"

Naklin claps his furry mitts.

We all run outside and call the Snow-nimals.

POP!

POOF!

POP!

The Snow-nimals come to life one after the other. They are no longer afraid.

We play another game of snow-berangs. Naklin can throw one halfway

around the WOM and back. Next we
make snow angels and build igloos!
Then Naklin spies my bed-sled.

"What is that?" he asks.

"Do you want to try it?" I offer. "Just jump on, and the bed-sled will do the rest."

The yeti sits on my bed-sled, and it creaks under his weight. When he slaps the covers like reins, it takes off.

"Uh-oh," Posey says.

I catch a snowflake on my tongue. "Uh-oh *what*-oh?" I ask, but I'm not sure I want to know the answer.

Posey looks in the direction Naklin took off. "Bed-sleds always go back to where they started," Posey explains.

Then my eyes bug out because I remember where it started . . . right under the door to my *bedroom*!

☆ Chapter Nine ☆

My *Room!*

I jump on Posey's bed-sled.

"Come on!" I shout. "Maybe we can catch him!"

Posey scrambles on board and we take off. We zoom to the door that leads to the Real World. My bed-sled is parked right below it. I look up, and sure enough, the door to the Real World hangs open—what's left of it.

Naklin nearly ripped the door off.

"Naklin!" I cry. Then I see something furry falling toward us. But it's not Naklin, it's Sir Pounce, and he's flying with all four legs sticking straight out. *FLUMP!* Sir Pounce lands on the bed with us.

"*MRRROW!*" that silly cat mews. I calm him down and look back up at the door, wondering how to get in. Then I see Naklin's big furry face appear in the broken doorframe.

"HELLO, DAISY AND AND-THIS-IS-POSEY!" calls the great yeti. "I OPENED MY FIRST DOOR!"

I stand on the bed-sled and wave my arms. "Move out of the way!" I cry. "We're coming up!" Then I ask Posey, "How do we get back up?"

He smiles. "Just bounce on the bed!"

I hold Sir Pounce as we bounce off the bed, and—ZOOP!—we're back in my room.

"DOORS ARE SO MUCH FUN!"
Naklin booms excitedly.

I put my fingers to my lips, hoping
he'll quiet down.

"Yes, and good job!" I whisper. "But

keep it down or my mom will hear."

That's when I see my room, and it's a total disaster. My bed is smashed! My dresser drawers are pulled out and cracked. My toys are everywhere!

Sir Pounce sniffs the debris.

"Is this your home?" asks Naklin.

What's left of it, I think, nodding.

"It's very small and much too warm for a yeti," he says. "May I go home now?"

My shoulders relax. What a relief!

"Of course," I say. "Adventures are fun, but it's always nice to go home."

Naklin gives Posey and me a very furry group hug. He smells fresh and chilly like a crisp winter day. Then we give him directions back to the Ice Castle.

Naklin sits down with his furry legs dangling through the open doorway.

"TOODLE-LOODLE-LOO!" the giant yeti shouts. Then he leaps through my floor.

"Toodle-loodle-loo!" Posey and I shout back as Naklin disappears into the WOM.

Then I hear a sharp knock on my real bedroom door.

Gadzooks! It's my mom! *Again!*

☆ Chapter Ten ☆

Posey's Trick

"Hold on!" I cry.

I was *supposed* to be cleaning my room this whole time, and now it's completely *trashed*. I can't tell Mom what happened. *Obviously.*

"Blankets!" Posey whispers.

We yank the blankets off my bed and throw them over the broken furniture and the hole in my floor. It looks like a super-amazing blanket fort! The mess is hidden, so I open the door.

"Welcome to Fort Blanket!" I say casually.

"Wow, Daisy, you're always full of surprises!" she says. "And I have a surprise for you, too!"

"Oooooh!" I cry. "I *love* surprises." Even though I've kind of had enough surprises for one day. *Obviously.*

"Lily and Jasmine are coming over for a snow day celebration!" she says. "Now make sure your room is picked up before they get here."

"No problem, Mom!" I say, pretending like it's no big deal. But as soon as she leaves, I can't pretend anymore. A yeti-smashed bedroom is

a very big deal. "Posey, my room is in *a million pieces*! What should I *do*?"

Posey leaps out from under one of the blankets.

"You wanna see a trick?" he asks.

I heave a big sigh. "No, not *now*," I tell him. "Not until this room is clean."

Posey starts his trick anyway. He claps his hands three times and throws one of my blankets over me.

"*Voilà!*" he shouts.

"Not funny," I grumble from under the blanket. But when I pull it off, my room is totally back to normal!

My furniture is fixed, my toys are put away, and my bed is made!

I twirl in a circle. "Posey, how did you *do* that?"

I give him a great big squeeze, and Posey laughs. "You said you didn't want to see the trick," he says.

Then he sits down by the open-
ing in the floor. "I should get going. I
want to visit Naklin and make sure he
got back to the Ice Castle. Those bed-
sleds can be tricky."

Now it's my turn to laugh. "Bring
earplugs this time!" I tell him.

"I will!" Posey says as he jumps through the door. "Bye, Daisy!"

"Bye!" I shout as the door closes and disappears. Now my floor is just a plain old floor again.

I stretch out on my bed and watch the snowflakes drift down. Sir Pounce is curled up next to me. Everything is falling-snow quiet.

This is the magic of a snow day.

Today is Friday, and that means it's park day! My best friends and I go to the park every Friday after school. Today we head straight to the basket-ball court.

I love the court because it's the best place to *ro-o-oll* on my skateboard.

Lily loves it because it's the best place to play basketball. And Jasmine loves it because it's the best place to draw on the smooth surface with sidewalk chalk. It's the perfect place for us. *Obviously.*

I slalom around Lily. *ZOOMIE! ZOOM! ZOOM!* She dunks a three-pointer or whatever.

I whiz past Jasmine. *ZOOMIE! ZOOM! ZOOM!* She's drawing a picture of Posey.

"Hi, Posey!" I shout as I fly by.

The picture of Posey pops to life—as in, *real* life.

"Hi, guys!" he shouts back.

I'm so distracted that I skate right into Lily.

WIPEOUT!

Lily and I bumble-tumble to the ground.

"Oopsy-daisy!" I cry. Lily and I untangle ourselves and check for scrapes.

"Are you okay?" everyone asks at the *exact same time*!

"JINX!" we shout, and then we crack up. We are *definitely* best friends.

Excerpt from *The Wishing-Well Spell*